This book belongs to

Phoebe and Chub

by Matthew Henry Hall
Illustrated by Sheila Aldridge

rising moon

www.risingmoonbooks.com

Composed in the United States of America
Printed in Malaysia

Edited by Theresa Howell
Designed by Katie Jennings
Production supervised by Donna Boyd

FIRST IMPRESSION 2005
ISBN 0-87358-879-7

Library of Congress Cataloging-in-Publication Data

Hall, Matthew Henry, 1965-
Phoebe and Chub / by Matthew Henry Hall ; illustrated by Sheila Aldridge.
p. cm.
Summary: A tree frog that lives in a creek at the bottom of a canyon and a fish
that lives in a river at the end of the creek become friends and play together every day.
[1. Tree frogs—Fiction. 2. Frogs—Fiction. 3. Fishes—Fiction. 4. Canyons—Fiction.
5. Friendship—Fiction.] I. Aldridge, Sheila, ill. II. Title.
PZ7.H1468Ph 2005
[E]—dc22
2004011711

Phoebe is a tree frog. She lives by a creek at the bottom of the canyon. Everyone along the creek knows Phoebe.

She has many friends.

One day Phoebe hopped and
splashed and swam all the way
down to where her little creek
rolls into the river.

There she met a fish named Chub.

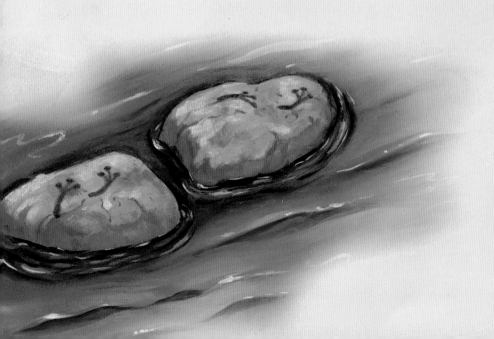

Phoebe and Chub became great friends. Most every day, Phoebe and Chub played together. They swam up the river and floated down the river, through rapids, and into other creeks.

Everywhere they went,
Phoebe and Chub made more friends.

Resting after a morning's swim,
Phoebe told Chub, "I wish I could fly."

Later that day, Chub told the dragonfly about Phoebe's wish.

Not long after that, the dragonfly told the lizard about Phoebe's wish.

The lizard told the coyote,
who told the snake,
who told the raven about Phoebe's wish.
The raven told the bighorn sheep,
who told the ground squirrel
about Phoebe's wish.

And that ground squirrel, who lived at
the very-very top of the canyon,
told the California condor
about Phoebe's
wish.

Not very long after this, it was Phoebe's birthday. Phoebe and her friends gathered by the river to sing songs, to play, and to eat birthday cake.

As the sun began to go down, Phoebe told Chub,
"This has been the best birthday ever!"
"It's not over yet," said Chub. "Remember when
you told me you wished you could fly?"

Chub whistled, and the condor flew over to them.

For my mother, my father, and my brother.

—M.H.H.

For Mom, who hails from the West.

—S.A.

A note from the author

PHOEBE HAS MANY FRIENDS. But many of her friends are *endangered*. Endangered means close to disappearing forever. Today, there are fewer than 200 California condors in the world and only a scattered number of bighorn sheep. Even Phoebe's best friend, Chub, and his relatives, the humpback chub, are endangered. Much work is being done to help these animals, but they need a lot more friends—people-friends—to survive. To learn more about endangered animals and how you can help, ask your librarian, teacher, or parents to help you look up books and other information.

Everybody—and everything—needs a friend.